A PRESENT FOR YOU

A PRESENT FOR YOU
BY MARGUERITA RUDOLPH

PICTURES BY JOHN E. JOHNSON

McGraw-Hill Book Company

New York • St. Louis • San Francisco • Düsseldorf
London • Mexico • Panama • Rio de Janeiro • Singapore
Sydney • Toronto

OTHER FIRST STEP BOOKS

I LIKE A WHOLE ONE by Marguerita Rudolph
illustrated by John E. Johnson

LOOK AT ME by Marguerita Rudolph
illustrated by Karla Kuskin

MOVING AWAY by Alice R. Viklund
illustrated by Reisie Lonette

SHARP AND SHINY by Marguerita Rudolph
illustrated by Susan Perl

To Trudy Finn—
who loves to give

Arthur was a little boy who was growing bigger and stronger. There were many things Arthur liked to do —staying overnight at his grandmother's, flying a kite with Daddy, and painting a chair with Mommy. Another thing Arthur liked was getting presents— especially surprise presents.

One morning Arthur was helping his mother take the groceries out of a shopping bag. He knew what everything was and where it belonged.

"A bunch of beets! A bag of carrots! Two cans of chicken soup!" Arthur was calling out. Then, "What's this?" he asked, pulling out a stapled bag. "What's inside?"

"Oh, that's a surprise," his mother answered.

"For me?" Arthur asked. His mother nodded.

Zip, swush, Arthur had the package opened in a second. Inside were a big drawing pad and a fat box of crayons. "That's the kind of paper and colors I *wanted!*"

"I like them myself," his mother said.

"Thank you," Arthur whispered, hugging his presents.

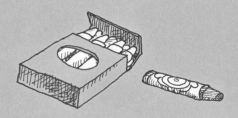

The next week, on his mother's birthday, Arthur's father came home with three brightly wrapped packages.

"Happy birthday, dear!" he said, and laid the packages in front of Mother. Arthur watched how she looked them over first and then slowly unwrapped them.

"Do it faster!" he said. "I want to see what's inside." But his mother kept unwrapping them very slowly. First the big package, which was a frame for one of her own paintings; then the little package, which was a string of tiny Indian beads. Finally she looked at the third—and her expression changed.

"This present is for you, Arthur," and she handed him a slim, straight package.

Arthur read his own name on it, and his eyes opened wide with surprise.

"Yippee!" He jumped into the air, then pulled off the wrapping. *Thump*, out fell a folded ruler. "That's the kind *you* have, Daddy! Will this one be mine?" *Push, click, push, click*—he already knew how it worked. "I didn't know I'd get a present on Mommy's birthday!" His father laughed.

"I thought you'd be surprised," he said.

Soon it was summer. Arthur and his mother were spending two weeks in a cottage by the beach. His father couldn't take a vacation at that time, so he stayed home and went to work.

Arthur liked their cozy cottage with his bunk bed inside and the smell of sweet honeysuckle outside. On the beach, he liked digging in the damp sand and getting sprayed with the slapping waves. But one thing bothered Arthur. He missed his father.

One morning when they were sunning on the beach, Arthur said:

"I want Daddy to come here for a few days!"

"He can't come now," his mother answered, "but maybe you can bring Daddy something from here."

"That's a good idea," agreed Arthur. "I'll do that." He jumped up and ran along the water's edge.

Soon he slowed down and began to look. Bright shells and smooth stones were in Arthur's path. Sand-pipers hopped and ran near the water. Arthur watched them, then he hopped and ran, too. When he looked up, Arthur noticed white sails gliding in the distance and sea gulls overhead.

As he walked back to where his mother was sketch-ing the water skiers, Arthur was thinking: "I wish I could bring Daddy a bird from the beach, but I could never catch one . . . A sailboat would be nice, but I couldn't bring him a real one!"

"Arthur!" his mother called to him. "I'm going to the village store—will you come with me?"

"Okay," he answered slowly. "Will you let me pull the wagon?"

"All right—you're big enough this year."

After Arthur's mother had bought the groceries and and had loaded them into the wagon, she said:

"Go look around the store, Arthur. You might see something you'd like to buy to bring home to Daddy."

"No," said Arthur. "I don't want to *buy* anything for Daddy! I want to *find* something."

The next morning, Arthur could hardly wait to get to the beach. Right after breakfast he made his bed, took out the garbage, and swept the cottage floor.

"Don't be a slowpoke, Mom," he called. "Get ready to go to the beach."

"Arthur, you're just too fast today."

When they came to the beach and Arthur's mother had settled down with a book, Arthur waved goodbye and ran off. He was in a mood to find something.

He skipped along the beach humming a song and looking here and there. Suddenly he stopped.

In front of him was a glistening greenish stone so beautiful that Arthur couldn't look at anything else. When he picked up the stone, it fit in the palm of his hand as if it belonged there. Arthur felt its weight. He rubbed his cheek against the stone. How smooth it was! He even licked it. It was the best thing he had ever found, and it gave him an idea. "I'll find another stone like it so I can bring one of them to Daddy." He held the stone snugly in his cupped hand, almost covering it with his fingers, and he kept looking for another stone.

He saw one that from a distance looked as round as a ball, but it had edges underneath, so he dropped it. He found one with bright specks, but it was too little, so he left it. Then he found a shiny black stone, very flat and very smooth. Arthur wanted it, and with his free hand put it in his pocket. Soon he noticed a pink stone, with a little white in it, and Arthur put it in his pocket. Then he picked up a gray-green one, then a small spotted one that looked like a bird's egg. Arthur's pocket was getting full, but none of the stones there was as beautiful as the one in his hand. When he saw a white stone that shone like the moon Arthur looked at it a long time—but finally he put it in his pocket with the others.

"Maybe," thought Arthur, "I can bring a collection of stones to daddy and he could pick out the one he likes best." Arthur kept finding more and more stones. When his pockets were full he put some stones inside his shirt, which was like a big pocket all around his waist. He held on to his shirt with one hand and held on to his special beauty of a stone with the other.

"What have you got?" his mother exclaimed as Arthur waddled up the beach to her. Without saying a word, Arthur emptied his pockets and his shirt front into his pail. *Clinkety-rackety* went the stones when they landed. And how wonderful they all looked together in the pail.

"Oh! Oh!" Arthur's mother kept saying as Arthur showed her first one stone and then another. She looked at each stone in the pail.

But there was still the special stone that Arthur held in his hand. "Let me see *that* one!" Arthur opened his hand. "Well! That *is* a beauty! It would make a wonderful paperweight."

Arthur now felt even more excited about finding it. He rubbed the stone on his pants before he slid it into his pocket.

"What are you going to do with all these stones?" his mother asked.

"I'll take them home — for Daddy," Arthur answered.

"Oh! That's a very nice present!" Mother said, "but stones are heavy, you know. We can't pack them in our suitcases."

Arthur had an answer to that problem.

"I'll choose the nicest stones only," he said.

"A good idea—and I'll help you choose them."

"No!" Arthur shook his head. "I want to choose them myself. And I'll carry them on the train in my pail—see?" Arthur held the pail full of stones with both hands.

As soon as they got back to the cottage Arthur looked over his collection and noticed that many of them looked alike. "I don't want three gray stones and four brown stones," he decided. So he put all the extra ones outside.

When he went to bed that night Arthur put the pail
of stones by his bunk, and the special stone under
his pillow.

The next morning, as soon as he woke up, he looked at it in the sunlight, and held it in his hand. After getting dressed, he put the stone snugly in his pocket.

This was the last day of their vacation and Arthur helped his mother with the packing. Then he looked over the stones and found more extra ones, which he put outside. His mother watched but she didn't tell Arthur which ones to choose.

"How many do you have now?" she asked. Arthur dumped them out and counted slowly.

"Fifteen!" Arthur answered, and put them one by one back into the pail.

When they were riding in the taxi to the railroad station Arthur took the special stone out of his pocket and held it in his hands.

"Is that still your favorite," Mother asked. Arthur nodded, and smiled at his mother. He just had time to put the stone safely back in his pocket before they boarded the train.

The ride home went very fast.

When the train came to the last stop, Arthur and his mother stepped onto the platform—Arthur with his pail, Mother with the suitcases. Arthur's father was waiting for them in the crowd. He waved and hurried towards them. They all hugged one another. Then Arthur's father noticed the pail.

"What wonderful stones! How did you ever find them?"

"I had to look for them. And *choose* them," Arthur explained.

"And I didn't help him," Mother added.

Then Arthur opened his hand where the shiny green stone was nesting. And his father's eyes opened wide with great surprise.

"This is my *favorite*," said Arthur. "You may hold it, Daddy!" Arthur's father looked at the stone and felt it in his hand.

"Very nice! And so smooth!" he said. "It would look great on a desk." Arthur was so happy to hear it that he suddenly wanted to give the stone to his father.

"It's *a present for you!*"

"For *me*?" his father asked. Arthur nodded. He was too excited about giving such a good present to answer. He surprised his father, his mother, and he surprised himself.

MARGUERITA RUDOLPH has worked for some 40 years as a nursery school teacher, director of child care centers and cooperative schools, as well as a college teacher. She is the author of three text books and numerous successful books for children including *The Traveling Frog, How A Shirt Grew in the Field, The Magic Sack,* and three First Step Books, *Look At Me, I Like A Whole One,* and *Sharp and Shiny.* Mrs. Rudolph is at present a Consultant in early childhood education and a full-time writer. She lives in Fresh Meadows, New York.

JOHN E. JOHNSON, illustrator of *I Like A Whole One,* has drawn the pictures for some forty books, most of them written for children, and his art has been selected for shows by the AIGA and the Society of Illustrators.

A graduate of the Philadelphia Museum school, Mr. Johnson lives on New York's upper west side with his wife and two children.